I Want My Child's Success in School

PRSE
of the Book

"This is an audacious and powerful read! This suggests us great parenting style which can mould children for great nation."

— Dr. VK Goswami
Visiting Scientist; UNIDO, ICTP, ITALY, Expert Panel, NOAA,
UNV, ICAO & AIU Rosters Vice Chancellor

"If you know anyone caring for someone facing certain problems regarding their children, this book could be the best gift ever."

— Dr. Ridwana Sanam
Founder & Managing Director (KRV Group) and Author of
"How to Write off Your Pain"

"If you are concerned about your child, read and follow this book. The book is worth reading and following."

— Colonel S.P. Singh
Author of "Personnel Administration"

This book is selected by National Book Trust(NBT), Government of India at:

▶ South Africa World Book Fair, 2012

▶ China World Book Fair, 2013

I WANT MY CHILD'S SUCCESS IN SCHOOL

Learn how to ensure your child's success through scientific tools and techniques

Gullybaba Publishing House Pvt. Ltd.

GULLYBABA PUBLISHING HOUSE PVT. LTD.
ISO 9001 & ISO 14001 Certified Co.
Regd. Office: 2525/193, 1st Floor, Onkar Nagar-A, Tri Nagar, New Delhi-110035 (Near Kanhaiya Nagar Metro Station)
Branch Office: 1A/2A, 20, Hari Sadan, Ansari Road, Daryaganj, New Delhi-110002
Ph.: 9350849407, 011-27387998
E-mail: info@gullybaba.com
Websites: GullyBaba.com, GullybabaKids.com

New Edition: 2019
ISBN: 978-93-81970-06-5

Contents

Few Words

Children are storehouses of talent, and all the children are unique. If encouraged and guided, they can shine in all aspects. They need to be encouraged ,and they seek unflagging support to succeed in school, and there is no better source for that support than from the family. Getting involved in your child's education can be rewarding for both you and your child.

To succeed in school and work, children need to know they are capable of doing a good job. Teachers working daily with students report that the most important 'school supply' a teenager can bring to school is a 'Can Do' attitude. As a parent, you play a major role not only in building confidence in your children, but reinforcing in them a constant spirit to win.

Help by encouraging them to do their 'personal best' in school and at home. Remember 'personal best' does not mean 'Perfect'; learning is not the same as high grades; and children, like adults, must be free to make mistakes and learn from them. Parents should talk about school each day. Ask to see class work, encourage your child to discuss new ideas and defend his or her opinions. Express your pride in their expressed views and demonstrated skills. Show interest and appreciation.

Expect your children to do their very best at school every day. Hold them accountable to complete their homework and work hard at school. Acknowledge them, appreciate them, correct them and stand by them. By helping your children believe they can be successful, they will be successful!

In the book, the word 'he' has been deliberately used for both boy and girl to avoid redundancy. The word 'he' does also include 'she'.

By following this book, you will help assure that your child has a successful school year.

– **Dinesh Verma**

Acknowledgements

I acknowledge the almighty GOD or universal energy which has brought precious words of wisdom in front of my eyes, the wisdom to touch the soul of those words and creativity to present some of them to parent in YOU.

Out of the large repository of words few words I would like to acknowledge:

When I first helped my newborn son, I looked at him
with tenderness and wondered and thought to myself,
you are the most precious gift from God. I don't own you.
I am here to help you find your way, to love you, and to
let you go.

Susie Risho, Mother of Three Grown Boys

And I am a practising parent trying to touch the soul of above words.

I would like to put in my appreciation and acknowledgement for my family members, relatives, friends and Team of Gullybaba Publishing House Pvt. Ltd. and GullybabaKids.com.

I convey my special thanks to all the kids with whom we experimented and played activities and all those who entertained and taught me.

No work can find success without the most important part, that is, YOU, The READERS. I wholeheartedly thank all those who took pain in the making of the book.

-Dinesh Verma

INTRODUCTION

"My children are the reason I laugh, smile and want to get up every morning."
~*Gena Lee Nolin*

Every child has the power to succeed in school and in life!!

Every parent; family member and caregiver can be a part of this growth and success. All the children are different individuals, and we first need to understand that each individual has unique qualities and habits. The individual strength and weaknesses of children can be identified. This can further help the children to be successful, and achieve success in school.

School-Parents have to work in harmony to ensure success of children in all the fields. Children spend a lot of time at school, and also imbibe a lot of values habits and culture in them. These values stay with them for a long time. Parents can be the key factor in the blending of these values with a positive attitude, to guide their children on the path of success.

Generally, children tend to do the same things as their parents do. What we say and do in our daily lives can help them to develop positive attitudes towards school and learning and to build confidence in themselves as learners. Showing our children that we both value education and use it in our daily lives provides them with powerful models and contributes greatly to their success in school.

As children's first and most important teacher, it's important that all parents build and keep strong ties to their children's schools. When parents and families are involved in their children's schools, the children do better and have better feelings about going to school. We can help our children to succeed by working with teachers to make sure that they provide curricula and use teaching methods that are based on strong scientific evidence about what works best in helping students to learn.

The purpose of this book is to make available to you information that you can use to help your child succeed in school. The book includes:

- information about things that you can do at home to contribute to your child's school success;

- activities that you can use to help your child acquire the skills to succeed in school;

- answers to often-asked questions about how to work with teachers; and

- tips on how to help your child with test taking.

The hours in a school day are many but the time a teacher can spend with any one child is limited. For children to be successful in school, parents and families need to be actively involved in their children's learning. They need to become involved early and stay involved throughout the school year. In fact, many studies show that what the family does is more important to a child's school success than how much money the family makes or how much education the parents have.

By showing interest in their children's education, parents and families can spark enthusiasm in them and lead them to a very important understanding—that learning can be enjoyable as well as rewarding and is well worth the effort required.

Co-curricular and Life Skills

Nowadays there are ample activities in school to monitor and gauge the overall success and performance of your child. The co-curricular activities such as dance/music/ sports/clubs are constantly providing a platform and opportunity to the children to perform well. The children are successful not only in academics, but in non-academic activities too.

Infact, their overall success depends largely on everything not only academics!!

Encourage your child to participate wholeheartedly in all school activities, assemblies, annual day programs!! It will give him a good learning experience and enable him to grow as a child!!

✗ ✗ ✗

"A nurturing parent protects and teaches their
child to survive and thrive inthekind of society
in which they will live."

THE BASICS

"At the end of the day, the most overwhelming key to a child's success is the positive involvement of parents."

~Jane D. Hull

If you think about it, although school is very important, it does not really take up very much of a child's time. In India, the school year averages 240 days; in other nations, the school year can last up to 180 days and students are often in school less hours per day than Indian students. Clearly, the hours and days that a child is not in school are important for learning too. Here are some things that you can do to help your child to make the most of that time:

Encourage your Child to Read

Helping your child become a reader is the single most important thing that you can do to help the child succeed in school — and in life. The importance of reading simply can't be undermined. Reading helps children in all school subjects. More importantly, it is the key to lifelong learning. Here are some tips on how to help your child become a reader. Here are some tips on how to help your child become a reader.

- Start early. When your child is still a baby, reading aloud to him should become part of your daily routine. At first, read for no more than a few minutes at a time, several times a day. As your child grows older, you should be able to tell if he wants you to read for longer periods. As you read, talk with your child. Encourage him to ask questions and to talk about the story. Ask him to predict what will come next. When your child begins to read, ask him to read to you from books or magazines that he enjoys.

- Keep lots of reading materials. Make sure that your home has lots of reading materials that are appropriate for your child. Keep books, magazines and newspapers in the house. Reading materials don't have to be new or expensive. You often can find good books and magazines for your child at yard or library sales. Ask family members and friends to consider giving your child books and magazine subscriptions as gifts for birthdays or other special occasions. Set aside quiet time for family reading. Some families even enjoy reading aloud to each other, with each family member choosing a book, story, poem or article to read to the others.

- Show that you value reading. Let your child see you reading for pleasure as well as for performing your routine activities as an adult — reading letters and recipes, directions and instructions, newspapers, computer screens and so forth. Go with him to the library and check out books for yourself. When your child sees that reading is important to you, he is likely to decide that it's important to him too.

  If you feel uncomfortable with your own reading ability or if you would like reading help for yourself or other family members, check with your local librarian or with your child's school about literacy programs in your community.

- Get help for your child if he has a reading problem. When a child is having reading difficulties, the reason might be simple to understand and deal with. For example, your child might have trouble seeing and need glasses or he may just need more help with reading skills. If you think that your child needs extra help, ask his teachers about special services, such as after-school or summer reading programs. Also ask teachers or your local librarian for names of community organizations and local literacy volunteer groups that offer tutoring services.

The good news is that no matter how long it takes; most children can learn to read. Parents, teachers and other professionals can work together to determine if a child has a learning disability or other problem and then provide the right help as soon as possible. When a child gets such help, chances are very good that he will develop the skills he needs to succeed in school and in life. *Nothing is more important than your support for your child as he goes through school. Make sure he gets any extra help he needs as soon as possible and always encourage him and praise him for his efforts.*

Talk to your Child

Talking and listening play major roles in children's school success. It's through hearing parents and family members talk and through responding to that talk that young children begin to pick up the language skills they will need if they are to do well. For example, children who don't hear a lot of talk and who aren't encouraged to talk themselves often have problems learning to read, which can lead to other school problems. In addition, **children who haven't learned to listen carefully often have trouble following directions and paying attention in class.**

Think of talking with your child as being like a tennis game with words — instead of a ball — bouncing back and forth. Find time to talk any place, for example:

- As you walk with your child or ride with him in a car or on a bus, talk with him about what he's doing at school. Ask him to tell you about a school assembly or a field trip. Point out and talk about things that you see as you walk — funny signs, new cars, and various people.

- As you shop in a store, talk with your child about prices, differences in brands and how to pick out good vegetables and fruit. Give your child directions about where to find certain items, and then have him go to get them.

- As you fix dinner, ask your child to help you follow the steps in a recipe. Talk with him about what can happen if you miss a step or leave out an ingredient.

- As you fix a sink or repair a broken table, ask your child to hand you the tools that you name. Talk with him about each step you take to complete the repair. Tell him what you're doing and why you're doing it. Ask him for suggestions about how you should do something.

- As you watch TV together, talk with your child about the programs. If you're watching one of his favorite programs, encourage him to tell you about the background of the characters, which ones he likes and dislikes and who the actors are. Compare the program to a program that you liked when you were at his age.

- As you read a book with your child, pause occasionally to talk to him about what's happening in the book. Help him to relate the events in the book to events in his life: "Look at that tall building! Didn't we see that when we were in Delhi?" Ask him to tell in his own words what the book was about. Ask him about new words in a book and help him to figure out what they mean.

It's also important for you to show your child that you're interested in what he has to say. Demonstrate for him how to be a good listener:

- When your child talks to you, stop what you're doing and pay attention. Look at him and ask questions to let him know that you've heard what he said: "So when are you going to help your granddad work on his car?"

- Ask him how can he help at home? What are the activities that the child likes to play at home, that involve all the members of the family.

- Let the child discuss what all happened at school or amongst his friends,and enjoy that experience. This will also lead to behavioral correction and increase closeness amongst the family members. The child can thus find a confidant in the members of his family,and feel secure.

- When your child tells you about something, occasionally repeat what he says to let him know that you're listening closely: "The school bus broke down twice!"

- You could also use this time to correct any grammatical or pronounciation errors that he makes.

Monitor Homework

Let your child know that you think education is important and so homework has to be done. Here are some ways to help your child with homework:

- **Have a special place for your child to study.**
  The homework area doesn't have to be fancy. A
  desk in the bedroom is nice, but for many
  children, the kitchen table or a corner of the living
  room works just fine. The area should have good
  lighting and it should be fairly quiet. Provide
  supplies and identify resources. For starters, make
  available pencils, pens, erasers, writing paper and
  a dictionary. Other supplies that might be helpful
  include a stapler, paper clips, maps, a calculator, a
  pencil sharpener, tape, glue, paste, scissors, a ruler,
  a calculator, index cards, and a dictionary. If
  possible, keep these items together in one place. If
  you can't provide your child with needed supplies,
  check with his teacher, school counselor or
  principal about possible sources of assistance.

- **Set a regular time for homework.** Having a
  regular time to do homework helps children to
  finish assignments on time. Of course, a good
  schedule depends in part on your child's age, as
  well as his specific needs. You'll need to work with
  a young child to develop a schedule. You should
  give your older child the responsibility for making
  up a schedule independently — although make
  sure that it's a workable one. You may find it
  helpful to have him write out his schedule and put
  it in a place where you'll see it often, such as on
  the refrigerator.

- **Remove distractions.** Turn off the TV and discourage your child from making and receiving social telephone calls during homework time. (A call to a classmate about an assignment, however, may be helpful). If you live in a small or noisy household, try having all family members take part in a quiet activity during homework time. You may need to take a noisy toddler outside or into another room to play. If distractions can't be avoided, your child may want to complete assignments in the local library.

- **Don't expect or demand perfection.** When your child asks you to look at what he's done — from skating a figure 8 to finishing a math assignment — show interest and praise him when he's done something well. If you have criticisms or suggestions, make them in a helpful way.

One final note: You may be reluctant to help your child with homework because you feel that you don't know the subject well enough or because you don't speak or read English as well as your child does. But helping with homework doesn't mean doing the homework. It isn't about solving the problems for your child; it's about supporting him to do his best. You may not know enough about a subject such as mathematics to help your child with a specific assignment, but you can help nonetheless by showing that you are interested, helping him get organized, providing a place for the materials he needs to work, monitoring his work to see that he completes it and praising his efforts.

Monitor TV Viewing and Video Game Playing

Indian children, on average, spend far more time watching TV or playing video games than they do completing homework or other school-related activities. Here are some suggestions for helping your child to use TV and video games wisely:

- Limit the time that you let your child watch TV. Too much television cuts into important activities in a child's life, such as reading, playing with friends and talking with family members.

- Model good TV viewing habits. Remember that children often imitate their parents' behavior.

Children who live in homes in which parents and other family members watch a lot of TV is likely to spend their time in the same way. Children who live in homes in which parents and other family members have "quiet" time away from the TV when they read (either alone to each other), talk to each other, play games or engage in other activities, tend to do the same.

- Watch TV with your child when you can. Talk with him about what you see. Answer his questions. Try to point out the things in TV programs that are like your child's everyday life.

- When you can't watch TV with your child, spot check to see what he's watching. Ask questions after the program ends. See what excites him and what troubles him. Find out what he has learned and remembered.

- Go to library and find books that explore the themes of the TV shows that your child watches.

- Limit the amount of time your child spends playing video games. As with TV programs, be aware of the games he likes to play and discuss his choices with him.

Encourage your Child to Use the Library

Libraries are places of learning and discovery for everyone. Helping your child find out about libraries will set him on the road to being an independent learner. Here are some suggestions for how to help:

- Introduce your child to the library as early as possible. Familiarise the children with books as early as possible.Even when your child is a toddler, take him along on weekly trips to the library. If you work during the day or have other obligations, remember that many libraries are open in the evening.

- If your child can print his name, it is likely that your library will issue him a library card if you will also sign for him. See that your child gets his own library card as soon as possible so that he can check out his own books.

- When you take your child to the library, introduce yourself and your child to the librarian. Ask the librarian to show you around the library and tell you about the services it has to offer. For example, in addition to all kinds of books, your library most likely will have magazines of interest to both your child and to you. It will likely to have newspapers from many different places. Most libraries also have tapes and CDs of books, music CDs and tapes, movies on video and on DVD and many more resources. Your library also might have books in languages other than Hindi/English or programs to help adults improve their English reading skills.

Ask the librarian to tell your child about special programs that he might participate in, such as summer reading programs and book clubs and about services such as homework help.

- Let your child know that he must follow the library's rules of behavior. Libraries want children to use their materials and services. However, they generally have rules such as the following that your child needs to know and obey:

  - Library materials must be handled carefully.

  - Materials that are borrowed must be returned on time. Your child needs to learn how long he can keep materials and what the fine will be for materials that are returned late.

  - All library users need to be considerate of each other. Shouting, running and being disruptive are not appropriate library behaviors.

Help your Child Learn to Use the Internet Properly and Effectively

The Internet/World Wide Web — a network of computers that connects people and information all around the world — has become an important part of how we learn and of how we interact with others. For children to succeed today, they must be able to use the Internet. Here are some suggestions for helping your child learn to do so properly and effectively:

- Spend time online with your child. If you don't have a computer at home, ask your librarian if the library has computers that you and your child may use. Learn along with your child. If you're not familiar with computers or with the Internet, ask the librarian if and when someone is available at the library to help you and your child learn together to use them.

  If your child knows about computers, let him teach you. Ask him to explain what he is doing and why. Ask him to show you his favorite websites and to tell you what he likes about them. This will help him build self- confidence and take pride in his abilities.

- Help your child locate appropriate websites. At the same time, make sure that he understands what you think are appropriate websites for him to visit. Point him in the direction of sites that can help him with homework or that relate to his interests.

Pay attention to any games he might download or copy from the Internet. Some games are violent or contain sexual or other content that is inappropriate for children. Resources such as GetNetWise (http://www.getnetwise.org/), a public service provided by Internet corporations and public interest groups and FamiliesConnect (http://www.familyconnect.org/parentsitehome.asp)can help you to make good Web site choices and give you more information about Internet use.

You might consider using "filters" to block your child from accessing sites that may be inappropriate. These filters include software programs that you can install on your computer. In addition, many Internet service providers offer filters (often for free) that restrict the sites that children can visit. Of course, these filters are not always completely effective — and children can find ways around them. The best safeguard is your supervision and involvement.

- Monitor the amount of time your child spends online. Internet surfing can be just as time consuming as watching TV. Don't let it take over your child's life. Have his place a clock near the computer and keep track of how much time he is spending online. Remember, many commercial online services charge for the amount of time the service is used. These charges can mount up quickly!

- Teach your child rules for using the Internet safely. Let him know that he should never do the following:

  - tell anyone — including his friends — his computer password;

  - use bad language or send cruel, threatening or untrue e-mail messages;

  - give out any personal information, including his name or the names of family members, home address, phone number, age, school name; or

  - arrange to meet a stranger that he has "talked" with in an online "chat room."

Encourage your Child to Be Responsible and to Work Independently

Taking responsibility and working independently are important qualities for school success. Here are some suggestions for helping your child to develop these qualities:

- **Establish rules.** Every home needs reasonable rules that children know and can depend on. Have your child help you to set rules, and then make sure that you enforce the rules consistently.

- **Give responsibility.** Make it clear to your child that he has to take responsibility for what he does, both at home and at school. For example, don't automatically defend your child if his teacher tells you that he is often late to class or is disruptive when he is in class. Ask for his side of the story. If a charge is true, let him take the consequences.

- **Develop a reasonable, consistent schedule.** Work with your child to develop a reasonable, consistent schedule of jobs to do around the house. List them on a calendar. Younger children can help set the table or put away their toys and clothes. Older children can help prepare meals and clean up afterwards.

- Show your child how to break a job down into small steps, then to do the job one step at a time. This works for everything — getting dressed, cleaning a room or doing a big homework assignment.

- Make your child responsible for getting ready to go to school each morning — getting up on time, making sure that he has everything he needs for the school day and so forth. If necessary, make a checklist to help him remember what he has to do.

- Monitor what your child does after school, in the evenings and on weekends. If you can't be there when your child gets home, give him the responsibility of checking in with you by phone to discuss his plans.

Encourage Active Learning

Children need active learning as well as quiet learning such as reading and doing homework. Active learning involves asking and answering questions, solving problems and exploring interests. Active learning also can take place when your child plays sports, spends time with friends, acts in a school play, plays a musical instrument or visits museums and bookstores.

✗ ✗ ✗

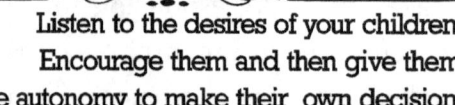

Listen to the desires of your children.
Encourage them and then give them
the autonomy to make their own decision.
~ Denis Waitley

ACTIVITIES

"The Golden Rule of Parenting is; do unto your children as you wish your parents had done unto you!"
~*Louise Hart*

What follows are activities that you can do with your child to help build the skills, attitudes and behaviors needed for school success. There is no one "right" way to do the activities. You should make changes and shorten or lengthen them to suit your child's attention span. You might want to use them as a starting point for some activities of your own. If you don't have some of the resources listed for an activity, remember that most public libraries offer free use of books, magazines, videos, computers and other services. Other things that you might need for these activities are not expensive.

Age levels for the activities are indicated at the start of each activity:

- **Ages 5-7**

- **Ages 7-9**

- **Ages 9-11**

Keep in mind, however, that children don't always learn the same things at the same pace. You are the best judge of what your child may be ready to try, so use the age levels as guides as your child learns and grows, not as hard and fast rules. For example, an activity listed for children ages 7-9 may work well with your 5-year-old. On the other hand, the same activity may not interest your child until he is 9 or 10.

As a parent, you can help your child to learn in a way no one else can. That desire to learn is a key to your child's later success. Enjoyment is important! So, if you and your child don't enjoy one activity, move on to another. You can always return to any activity later on.

Can Parents Top This?
(For children ages 5 to 7)

Learning to take turns helps your child build spoken language skills as well as work with others.

What Can Parents Do?

- With your child, make up a story for the two of you to tell together, taking turns saying one sentence at a time.

  - Begin by deciding on a topic, such as *pirates*.

  - Say the first sentence: "Once upon a time a pirate lived in . . ."

  - Continue taking turns with your child making up and telling parts of the story until you decide to end it — maybe after eight or ten sentences.

- Take turns beginning and finishing a story. Ask other family members and friends to join in.

Working with others, listening to what they say and making good contributions are all valuable in helping children to complete school projects.

Listen!
(For children ages 5 to 7)

Listening to and giving directions helps your child to sharpen listening and speaking skills.

What Parents Need?

- Any small object, such as a ball or a photograph

- Objects that can make noise, such as keys, water glasses, spoons and decks of cards

What Can Parents Do?

- Hide a small object. Give your child directions to find it such as, "Take five steps straight ahead. Turn right. Keep the lamp to your left. Bend down and look to the right." Next, have your child hide the object and give you directions to find it.

- Have your child close his eyes. Use something to make a sound, such as rattling your keys, tapping a spoon against a glass or riffling a deck of cards. Ask your child to guess what's making the sound.

- Clap your hands to tap out a rhythm. Have your child listen and then clap that same rhythm back to you. Make the rhythms harder as he catches on.

- Take a walk with your child. Find a place to sit for a few minutes and both close your eyes for 30 seconds or so. Tell each other what you hear: a baby crying, an airplane, a bird singing, cars on the street, leaves rustling.

- Take a walk with your child. This time, take turns telling each other what to do: cross the street, turn left, look down

For success in school, children need to learn to listen carefully, to see and hear details and to follow and give clear directions.

It's a Match
(For children ages 5 to 7)

Sorting and classifying helps your child to pay attention to details and recognize how things are alike and different.

What Parents Need?
- Dishes, flatware, glasses
- Laundry

What Can Parents Do?
- As you empty the dishwasher or wash and dry dishes, ask your child to make stacks of dishes that are of the same size, to put glasses that are of the same size together and to sort forks, knives and spoons.

- As you empty the clothes dryer, ask your child to match pairs of socks or to put all white things together, all blue things and so forth.

Encourage your child to participate wholeheartedly in all school activities, assemblies, annual day programme!! It will give him a good learning experience and enable him to grow as a child!!

Let's Read
(For children ages 5 to 7

Reading is the single most important way for your child to develop the knowledge needed to become successful in school.

What Parents Need?
- Children's books that your child can read
- Books of riddles, tongue twisters and silly rhymes.

What Can Parents Do?
- Read with your child. Take turns, with you reading one page or paragraph and your child reading the next. You might also read the parts of different characters in a story. Be enthusiastic

about reading. Read the story with expression. Make it more interesting by talking as the characters would talk, making sound effects and using facial expressions and gestures. Encourage your child to do the same.

- Help your child to read new words by having him use what he knows about letters and the sounds they make to sound out the words.

- If he is unsure of the meaning of a word, help him to use the surrounding words or sentences to figure it out. If this doesn't help, just tell him what the word means and keep reading.

- Buy a children's dictionary if possible — one that has pictures next to the words. Then start the "let's look it up" habit.

When reading is a regular part of family life, parents and families send their children a message that it is important, enjoyable and a great way to learn.

Author! Author!
(For children ages 5 to 7)

Reading and writing support each other. The more your child does any of these, the better he will be at both.

What Parents Need?

- Pencils, crayons or markers

- Writing paper

- Cardboard or heavy paper

- Construction paper

- Safety scissors

- Yarn or ribbon

What Can Parents Do?

- Write with your child. Talk with him about your writing so that he begins to understand that writing means something and has many uses.

- Hang a family message board in the kitchen. Offer to write notes there for your child. Be sure that he finds notes there for him.

- Help your child write notes or e-mails to relatives and friends to thank them for gifts or to share his thoughts. Encourage the relatives and friends to answer your child.

- As your child gets older, he can begin to write you longer stories. Ask questions that will help him organize the stories. Answer questions about spelling.

- Help your child to turn his writing into books. Paste his drawings and writings on pieces of construction paper. For each book, have him make a cover out of heavier paper or cardboard, then add special art, a title and his name as author. Punch holes in the pages and cover and bind the book together with yarn or ribbon.

Writing helps children to organize their thoughts and gives them an important way to communicate with others.

Now You See It, Now You Don't
(For children ages 5 to 7)

Doing simple science experiments at home can prepare your child to learn important science concepts — and the need to be patient.

What Parents Need?
- 2 ice cube trays

- Clock

- Small bowls

- Paper and pencil

- Water and other liquids, such as fruit juices

What Can Parents Do?

- Give your child a pencil and paper and tell him that he is going to be a scientist and take notes about what he observes in some experiments.

- Together with your child, fill one ice cube tray to the top with water. Fill the other tray only half full. Put both trays in the freezer. Have your child record the time. Tell him to watch the clock and check every 30 minutes or so to see if the water in each tray has frozen (if not, wait until it has frozen).

    - Ask your child to write down how long it took the water in each tray to freeze.

    - Ask him which amount of water froze faster? Invite him to explain why he thinks this happened.

- Have your child take one ice cube from each tray and put them in separate bowls to melt. Ask him to write down which cube melts faster — the larger or the smaller one.

- Put one ice cube in a window and another in the refrigerator (not the freezer) and have your child write down how long they each take to melt.

- Freeze samples of liquids such as different kinds of fruit juices. Have your child compare their freezing times to that of water.

Careful observation and note taking are valuable school skills.

How much does It Weigh?
(For children ages 5 to 7)

Build your child's interest in math and science by helping him to observe, estimate and weigh objects at home.

What Parents Need?
- Bathroom scale

- Objects to weigh, such as bags of sugar, flour, potatoes or onions; boxes of cereal and cookies; shoes of different sizes

- Paper and pencil

What Can Parents Do?
- Show your child two objects such as a five-pound bag of sugar and a ten-pound bag of potatoes and ask him to guess which weighs more. Show him how to use a scale to weigh the objects. Have him record the weights.

- Next, show him several objects and ask him to guess how much each weighs. Have him write his estimates, and then weigh the objects.

- If you choose, have your child estimate his own weight, as well as that of other family members and use the scale to check his guesses.

The use of simple bathroom and kitchen scales at home prepares children for using equipment in school to weigh and measure.

Start to Finish
(For children ages 5 to 7)

Organization has to be learned. Help your child learn to plan, begin and finish a job.

What Parents Need?
- Pencil and paper

- Items used to do a job around the house, such as watering plants or setting the table.

What Can Parents Do?
- Together with your child, select a job he usually does around the house, such as watering the plants. Ask him to make a chart like the one below, then write down or tell you the "Plan," "Do," and "Finish" steps needed to do his job well. Look over these steps together and talk about possible changes.

Plan	Do	Finish
Get supplies 1. watering can 2. paper towel	1. fill can 2. water plants 3. wipe up spills 4. pick off dead leaves	1. throw away used towels and dead leaves 2. put away can

- List the "Plan," "Do," and "Finish" steps of one or two jobs that you do around the house. Ask your child to help you think of ways that you can improve each step.

- When you give your child a new task, help him to plan the steps so that he can do the job well and have a sense of accomplishment.

Students who can plan a task are usually more successful and can do it in a shorter amount of time.

Where did I Put That?
(For children ages 7 to 9)

Older children also need help getting organized. Creating a special place for school items will help make mornings smoother for both your child and you.

What Parents Need?

- Cardboard box

- Crayons or markers

What Can Parents Do?

- Find a sturdy cardboard box or carton large enough to hold notebooks and other school things. Let your child decorate it with pictures, words or artwork and his name. Agree with the child about where to put the box. You might suggest a spot near the front door or the place where he does homework.

- Let your child know that his school things should go in the box as soon as he comes home from school. All homework and anything else he needs for school the next day also should go into it.

- Let your child make a rainy day box and put it in a different place (or make it a different color). Have him fill it with "treasures" — games, books, photographs, souvenirs and keepsakes. Invite other members of the family to put surprises in the box from time to time (no snakes or frogs, please!).

- Show your appreciation when your child keeps things in order.

Keeping all school items in one place helps teach children how much easier life can be when they are organized and plan ahead.

My Place
(For children ages 7 to 9)

Children tend to argue over the same space (even in a big room). By having an area of the floor marked off, each child has a place that feels like his own.

What Parents Need?

- Space — even a tiny area will do

- Small table

- Chair

- Lamp

- Small floor covering

What Can Parents Do?

- Find a quiet study area away from the TV and radio for each child (even those not old enough to have homework yet).

- Put a rug or a section cut from an old blanket or sheet on a small area of the floor. Use this to mark off each child's private study space. Put the table and chair on the floor covering. This space does not have to be in the same place all the time. If the table is lightweight, the floor covering can be put down any place it is out of the way (such as near the kitchen if a child needs help as you are fixing dinner). It can also be put away when it is not being used.

- If the study space will always be in the same place, let the child try out different arrangements of the furniture to see what works best. Make sure he arranges the lamp so that the study area is well lit.

- Have him label items with his name.

Having a special place at home helps children to focus on what they are studying.

Making Money
(For children ages 7 to 9)

Help your child learn about money.

What Parents Need?
- Dice

- One rupee coins, five rupee coins, ten rupee coins

What Can Parents Do?

- This is a good game to play with the family. Have each player roll the dice and say the number. Then give the player that number of one rupee coins.

- When a player gets 5 one rupee coins, replace them with a five rupee coin. When he gets 2 five rupee coins, replace them with a ten rupee coin.

- The first player to reach the set amount — 25 or 50 rupees, for example — wins.

Children can be confused by money. Some might think that the larger a coin the more valuable it is. Playing counting games at home can be valuable in helping children deal with numbers and math concepts in school.

Reading on the Go
(For children ages 7 to 9)

Show your child that reading has value in everyday life.

What Parents Need?

- Map of your areas

- Bus, subway and/or train schedules for your area

What Can Parents Do?

- Help your child use a map to mark a route to a special place, such as his school, the football stadium, the mall or his grandmother's house. Help him to figure out the distance to the place.

- Next, give him a bus, subway or train schedule and have him find departure and arrival times and the rates. Have him figure out how long the trip takes and how much it costs.

Children need to learn that reading is not just something they do in school — it is important in all parts of their lives.

My Time Line
(For children ages 7 to 9

You can help your child use events in his own life to gain both a sense of time and to understand the order in which things happen.

What Parents Need?
- Shelf paper
- Yardstick
- Pencils, makers or crayons

What Can Parents Do?
- Place a long piece of shelf paper on the floor. Have your child use a yardstick to draw a line that is three feet long.

- Talk with your child about important dates in his life — the day he was born; his first day of kindergarten, of first grade; the day his best friend moved in next door and so forth. Tell him to write the dates on the line. Invite him to add dates that are important for the whole family — the day his baby brother/sister was born, the day his favorite aunt got married — and the dates of any important historical events.

- Display the finished time line and ask your child to tell other family members and friends what it shows.

Making and reading time lines helps children to learn about the flow of history and to develop an understanding of cause and effect.

Time Flies
(For children ages 9 to 11)

"I don't have time to do that!" Sound familiar? Planning time is one of the most useful things that your child can learn. Knowing how long something will take can save time and avoid last minute hassles.

What Parents Need?

- Paper and pencil
- Clock
- Calendar

What Can Parents Do?

- Together with your child, write down estimates of how long it takes each of you to do certain tasks (such as getting ready for school or work in the morning; ironing clothes; making toast). Use a clock to time at least one of these tasks. Then take turns timing each other. (Be realistic — it's not a race).

- Talk with your child what part of a job can be done ahead of time, such as deciding the eatable in his breakfast and lunch at bedtime.

- Talk about at least two places that you and your child go where you must be on time. What do you do to make sure you are on time?

Being on time or not being on time affects other people. It is important for children to understand their responsibility for being on time — it's not just for grown-ups.

Homework made Easy
(For children ages 9 to 11)

A homework chart can show your child exactly what he needs to do and when he needs to do it.

What Parents Need?

- Poster board or large sheet of sturdy paper

- Marker, pen or pencil

- Clock

What Can Parents Do?

- Help your child to create a homework chart like the following out of a large piece of sturdy paper:

Subject	Mon.	Tues.	Wed.	Thurs.	Fri.
Language Arts					
Social Science					
Math					
Science					

Depending on how many subjects your child has, he may be able to put three or four weeks on each piece of paper.

- Help him to attach a colored marker or pen to the chart so that it is always handy.

- After school each day, have your child put a check mark in each box in which there is a homework assignment. Circle the check when you have seen that the homework is completed.

- Tell your child to try to figure out how long it will take him to complete each homework assignment so that he could be able to schedule his time.

Children need to know that their family members think homework is important. If they know their families care, children have a good reason to complete assignments on time.

Divide and Conquer
(For children ages 9 to 11)

Anything is easier to do if it's divided into smaller pieces. As your child's assignments get longer and more complicated, he needs to acquire more organizing and planning skills.

What Parents Need?
- Homework assignments
- Chores
- Paper
- Pencil

What Can Parents Do?
- Have your child choose a big homework assignment to talk about, such as a geography

project. Sit with him and help him make a list of what he needs to complete the job. For example:

Reference materials (books, maps)

Ask: Can you complete the assignment by just using your textbook? If not, do you need to go to the library? If so, can you check out books or will you have to allow time to stay there and use reference books? Can you use websites? Do you have the addresses for approved sites? Does your teacher have them?

Taking notes

Do you have a notebook? Pencils?

Finished project

Can you do this assignment on a computer? Will you need to staple the pages together? Do you need a report folder or cover? Do you need to draw pictures or make charts? Can you use computer graphics?

- Help your child decide the order in which the parts of the job need to be done. Let him number them.

To help him estimate how long each part of the assignment will take, tell him to work backward from the date the assignment is due. Have him figure out how much time he'll need to complete each part. Have him write down start and finish dates next to each part.

- Have him put the assignment dates on a calendar or his homework chart.

- Together, think about a household job, such as cleaning out a closet or mowing the yard. Help your child to divide it up into smaller parts.

- Talk with your child about how you divide work at your job or at home.

Learning to see assignments or big jobs in small pieces can make them less overwhelming for a child.

Help Wanted
(For children ages 9 to 11)

Older children are interested in life beyond school. You can help your child to have a realistic sense of that life and what he can do to prepare for it.

What Parents Need?
- Pencil and paper
- Newspaper help-wanted ads

What Can Parents Do?
- Talk with your child about what he wants to be and do in the future. Ask, for example, "What job

do you think you'd like to do when you get out of school? What kind of education or training do you think you'll need to get this job?"

- Suggest that your child pick two adults he knows, such as neighbors or relatives, to talk with briefly about their jobs. Help him to think of at least three questions to ask. Have him write the questions, leaving space for the answers. Here are some sample questions:

  - What is your job?
  - How long have you had it?
  - Do you like it?
  - Did you need to go to college to get your job?
  - Did you require to have any special training?
  - What kind of classes do I need to take in high school for a job like yours?

- After the interview, talk with your child about what he learned.

- Next, show your child the newspaper help wanted ads. Have him find ads for three jobs that he might want to have in the future. Have him read aloud the requirements for a job and talk with him about the skills, education and training he would need to have to do the work.

Jobs change dramatically over time and the job that your child is interested in now may not even exist in the future. Help him/her to understand that it is important to be well educated and open-minded so that he/she can be flexible.

TV Time
(For children ages 9 to 11)

Watching television can be educational for your child or just something that she does to fill the time.

What Parents Need?

- TV set

- World map

- Reference books (or online Web news, biography and geography sites)

What Can Parents Do?

- Place a world map next to the TV set. Arrange to watch TV news programs with your child.

- After the program have your child use the map to find world news spots.

- Have your child use reference books such encyclopedias or appropriate websites to find out more information about a story, a country or a person in the news.

Good TV programs can spark children's curiosity and open up new world to them.

We must also Pay Attention on

Enforce Healthy Habits

You can't perform well when you don't feel good. To help your child have the best chance at doing well in school, make sure she follows healthy habits at home. Choose a bedtime that will give your child plenty of sleep, and provide a healthy breakfast each morning. Encourage exercise, and limit the amount of time she spends watching TV, playing video games, listening to music, or using the computer.

Read, Again and Again

It is often said that children spend the first several years learning to read, and the rest of the lives reading to learn. The written word is a gateway to all kinds of learning, and the more you read to your child, the better chance he has of becoming an eager and proficient reader.

Try to sit down with your child to read a little bit every day, give him plenty of opportunities to read out loud to you, as well, and above all have fun. While the importance of reading with your child cannot be stressed enough, it should not be the cause of stress.

Take the Lead

Children learn by example. Let your kids "catch" you reading. Take time to learn a new skill and discuss the experience with them. Sit down and pay bills or do other "homework" while your kids do their schoolwork.

If you display a strong work ethic and continually seek out learning opportunities for yourself, your kids will begin to model that same behavior in their own lives.

Talk Often

Do you know how your child feels about his classroom, his teacher, and his classmates? If not, ask his. Talk with him about what he likes and doesn't like at school. Give him a chance to express his anxieties, excitements, or disappointments about each day, and continue to support and encourage him by praising his efforts and achievements.

Show Interest

Don't limit your support to your child; extend it to his teachers as well. Meet the teachers and stay in regular contact by phone or e-mail so that you can discuss any concerns as they arise. Not only will it pave the way for you to ask questions, but it will also make the teachers more comfortable with calling you if they have concerns about your child.

Expect Success

Perhaps the most important way through which you can support your child's efforts at school is to expect him to succeed. That doesn't mean that you demand he be the best student, or the best athlete or the best artist. Rather, let him know that you expect him to do "his best" so that he'll be proud of what he can accomplish.

If you make that expectation clear and provide a home environment that promotes learning, then your child will have a greater chance of becoming the best student he can be.

✗ ✗ ✗

Happiness is when...

you realize your children have turned out to be good people.

 WORKING WITH
TEACHERS AND
SCHOOLS

"The relation between parents and children is essentially based on teaching."
~*Gilbert Highet*

Many teachers say that they don't often receive information from parents about problems at home. Many parents say that they don't know what the school expects from their children — or from them. Sharing information is essential and both teachers and parents are responsible for making it happen. The following questions and answers can help you to get the most out of talking to your child's teacher or with other school staff members.

Q: What do parents do first?

Learn everything that you can about your child's school. The more you know, the easier your job as a parent will be. Ask for a school handbook. This will answer many questions that may arise over the year. If your school doesn't have a handbook, ask questions. Ask the principal and teachers, for example: What classes does the school offer? Which classes are required? What are your expectations for my child? How does the school measure student's progress? Does it meet state standards? What are the school's rules and regulations?

Ask about specific teaching methods and materials — are the methods based on evidence about what works best in teaching reading or math? Are the science and history textbooks up to date?

Ask if the school has a website and, if so, get the address. School websites can provide you with read access to all kinds of information — schedules of events, names of people to contact, rules and regulations and so forth.

Keep informed throughout the school year. If your schedule permits, attend PTA meetings. If you are unable to attend, ask that the minutes of the meetings be sent to you. Or, find out if the school makes these minutes available on its website.

Q:When should parents talk with their child's teacher?

Early and often. Contact your child's teacher or teachers at the beginning of the year or as soon as you can. Get acquainted and show your interest.

Tell teachers what they need to know about your child. If he has special needs, make these known from the beginning.

If you notice a big change in your child's behavior, school performance or attitude during the school year, contact the teacher immediately.

Report cards are one indication of how well your child is doing in school. But you also need to know how things are going between report cards. For example, if your son is having trouble in math, contact the teacher to find out when he has his next math test and when it will be returned to him. This allows you to address a problem before it mushrooms into something bigger. Call the teacher if your son/daughter doesn't understand an assignment or if he needs extra help to complete an assignment. You may also want to find out if your child's teachers use e-mail to communicate with parents. Using e-mail will allow you to send and receive messages at times that are most convenience for you.

Q: What parents should do if their children have problems in doing their homework?

Contact the teacher as soon as you suspect that your child has problem with his schoolwork. Schools have a responsibility to keep you informed about your child's performance and behavior and you have a right to be upset if you don't find out until report-card time that your child is having difficulties. On the other hand, you may figure out that a problem exists before the teacher does. By alerting the teacher, you can work together to solve a problem in its early stages.

Request a meeting with the teacher to discuss problems. Tell him briefly why you want to meet. You might say, "Rohan is having trouble with his social studies' homework. I'm worried about why he can't finish the assignments and what we might do to help him." If English is your second language, you may need to make special arrangements, such as including in the meeting someone who is bilingual.

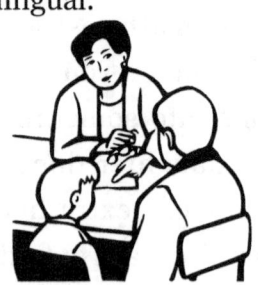

Approach the teacher with a cooperative spirit. Believe that the teacher wants to help you and your child, even if you disagree about something. Don't go to the principal without first giving the teacher a chance to work out the problem with you and your child.

Q:How do parents get the most out of parent-teacher conferences?

Be prepared to listen as well as to talk. It helps to write out questions before you leave home. Also jot down what you want to tell the teacher. Be prepared to take notes during the conference and ask for an explanation if you don't understand something.

In conferences, the teacher should offer specific details about your child's work and progress. If your child has already received some grades, ask how your child is being evaluated.

Talk about your child's talents, skills, hobbies, study habits and any special sensitivity such as concern about weight or speech difficulties.

Tell the teacher if you think your child needs special helps and about any special family situation or event that might affect your child's ability to learn. Mention such things as a new baby, an illness or a recent or an upcoming move.

Ask about specific ways to help your child at home. Try to have an open mind.

At home, think about what the teacher has said and then follow up. If the teacher has told you that your child needs to improve in certain areas, check back in a few weeks to see how things are going.

Q: What should be done If parents do not agree with the school rule or with a teacher's assignments?

First, don't argue with the teacher in front of your child. Set up a meeting to talk about the issue. Before the meeting, plan what you are going to say — why you think a rule is unfair or what exactly you don't like about an assignment. Get your facts straight and don't rely on anger to win your argument. Try to be positive and remain calm. Listen carefully.

If the teacher's explanation doesn't satisfy you, arrange to talk with the principal or even the school superintendent. Do not feel intimidated by titles or personalities. An educator's primary responsibility is to ensure the success of each and every student in his classroom, school or district.

Q: What's the best way for parents to stay involved in their children's school activities?

Attend school events. Go to sports events and concerts; attend back-to-school night, parent-teacher meetings and awards events, such as a "perfect attendance" breakfast.

Volunteer in your school. If your schedule permits, look for ways to help out at your child's school. Schools often send home lists of ways in which parents can get involved. Chaperones are needed for school trips or dances (and if your child thinks it's just too embarrassing to have you on the dance floor, sell soft drinks down the hall from the dance). School committees need members and the school newsletter may need an editor. The school may have councils or advisory committees that need parent representatives. If work or other commitments make it impossible for you to volunteer in the school, look for ways to help at home. For example, you can make phone calls to other parents to tell them about school-related activities or maybe help translate a school newsletter from English into another language.

Q: What if parents don't have time to volunteer as much as they would like?

Even if you can't volunteer to do work at the school building, you can help your child learn when you're at home. The key question is, "What can I do at home easily and in a few minutes a day, to reinforce and extend what the school is doing?" This is the involvement that every family can and must provide.

The schools also need to take steps so that parents feel good about what they're doing at home and know they're helping.

✗ ✗ ✗

THE solution to every
parenting problem starts
with nine little words:
'I'm here.'
'I hear you.'
'How can I help?'

HELPING YOUR CHILD WITH TEST-TAKING

"The well-being and welfare of children should always be our focus."
~Todd Tiahrt

You can be a great help to your child if you will observe these do's and don'ts about tests and testing:

- Do talk to your child about testing. It's helpful for children to understand why schools give tests and to know the different kinds of tests they will take.

  Explain that tests are yardsticks that teachers, schools, school districts and even states use to measure what and how they teach and how well students are learning what is taught. Most tests are designed and given by teachers to measure students' progress in a course. These tests are associated with the grades on report cards. The results tell the teacher and students whether they are keeping up with the class, need extra help or are ahead of other students.

The results of some tests tell schools that they need to strengthen courses or change teaching methods. Still other tests compare students by schools, school districts or cities. All tests determine how well a child is doing in the areas measured by the tests.

Tell your child that occasionally, he will take "standardized" tests. Explain that these tests use the same standards to measure students' performance across the state or even across the country. Every student takes the same test according to the same rules. This makes it possible to measure each student's performance against that of others.

• Do encourage your child. Praise him for the things that he does well. If your child feels good about himself, he will do his best on a test. Children who are afraid of failing are more likely to become anxious when taking tests and more likely to make mistakes.

- Do meet with your child's teacher as often as possible to discuss his progress. Ask the teacher to suggest activities for you and your child to do at home to help prepare for tests and to  improve your child's understanding of schoolwork.

- Do make sure that your child attends school regularly. Remember, tests reflect children's overall achievement. The more effort and energy your child puts into learning, the more likely it is that he will do well on tests.

- Do provide a quiet, comfortable place for studying at home and make sure that your child is well rested on school days and especially on the day of a test. Children who are tired are less able to pay attention in class or to handle the demands of a test.

- Do provide books and magazines for your child to read at home. By reading new materials, a child will learn new words that might appear on a test. Ask your child's teacher for lists of books for outside reading or get suggestions from your local library.

- Don't get upset because of a single test score. Many things can influence how your child does on a test. He might not have felt well on test day or he might have been too nervous to concentrate. He might have had an argument with a friend before the test or he might have been late to school because the school bus got struck in traffic. Remember, one test is simply one test.

- Don't place so much emphasis on your child's test scores that you lose sight of his well being. Too much pressure can affect his test performance. In addition, he may come to think that you will only love him if he does well on tests.

- Do help your child avoid test anxiety. It's good for your child to be concerned about taking a test. It's not good for him to develop "test anxiety." Test anxiety is worrying too much about doing well on a test. It can mean disaster for your child. Students with test anxiety can worry about success in school and about their future success. They can become very self-critical and lose confidence in their abilities. Instead of feeling challenged by the prospect of success, they become afraid of failure. If your child worries too much about taking tests, you can help to reduce the anxiety by encouraging the child to do the following things:

  - Plan ahead. Start studying for the test well in advance. Make sure that you understand what material the test will cover. Try to make connections about what will be on the test and what you already know. Review the material more than once.

- Don't "cram" the night before. This might increase your anxiety, which will interfere with clear thinking. Get a good night's sleep.

- When you get the test, read the directions carefully before you begin to answer the questions. If you don't understand how to do something, ask the teacher to explain.

- Look quickly at the entire text to see what types of questions are on it (multiple choice, matching, true/false, essay). See if different questions are worth different numbers of points. This will help you to determine how much time to spend on each part of the test.

- If you don't know the answer to a question, skip it and go on. Don't waste time worrying about one question. Mark it and, if you have time at the end of the test, return to it and try again.

After the Test

Your child can learn a great deal from reviewing a graded exam paper. Reviewing will show him where he had difficulty and, perhaps, why. This is especially important for classes in which the material builds from one section to the next, as in math. Students who have not mastered the basics of math, are not likely to be able to work with fractions, square roots, beginning algebra and so on.

Discuss the wrong answers with your child and find out why he chose the (wrong) answers. He may have misunderstood or misread a question. Or, he may have known the correct answer but failed to make his answer clear. Sometimes, handwriting also happens to be a big culprit for poor score.

You and your child should read and discuss all comments that the teacher writes on a returned test. If any comments aren't clear, tell your child to ask the teacher to explain them.

✗ ✗ ✗

PROMOTE ACTIVE
LEARNING

"Listen to the desires of your children. Encourage
them and then give them the autonomy to make their
own decision."
~Denis Waitley

To promote active learning, listen to your child's ideas
and respond to them. Let him jump in with
questions and opinions when you read books together.
When you encourage this type of give-and-take at home,
your child's participation and interest in school is likely to
increase.

Here are some tips that parents can use to help their children be successful in school.

- **Get a plan and stick to it:** Set a specific "quiet
  time" every day for homework or general reading.
  Involve your child in setting the rules for this. Ask
  your child to come up with 3 rules — for example:

- Collect all needed materials before starting.

- No talking or fooling around during quiet time.

- Complete all work before stopping.

  Write the rules on paper and post them in your house. Children are more likely to follow rules that they helped create.

  Some elementary school students have 20 30 minutes a day set aside for this purpose. Junior and senior high school students may need at least 30-45 minutes for daily study time. Some schools expect students to spend at least 15 minutes per subject each day on homework. Check with the teachers to see how much homework to expect for your child.

  Homework, even if routine, should not be viewed as optional, any more than is an assignment or project at your place of work.

- **Be a cheerleader:** Some children do poorly in school because they see themselves as unworthy. For a child to feel good about learning, he must first feel good about himself. Encourage your child by praising him for his efforts. Express interest in his school work.

- **Make no excuses:** Avoid giving your child a reason for making excuses. Even if you think your child will feel better if you do so, never say this sort of thing: "Some people just don't have a head for math." Your child may think that you think: he isn't able to handle a task. Success in a future job will require your child do the best she can. You will not help your child by encouraging his to make excuses whenever it is convenient.

- **Light a fire:** Be enthusiastic! It can be contagious. Don't give the message that homework is a boring chore. Children who do well, enjoy learning. If your child does not seem motivated to do well in school, try to find ways to make the learning fun.

- **Make learning "real":** The best learning is hands-on. Show how school work skills are needed and used in day-to-day life. For example, a child who helps make a meal learns fractions, telling time, reading and multi-step problem solving. Show your child what is under the hood when you work on the car. Ask for "help" when you balance the checkbook or write "thank you" notes and letters. Have your child jot down notes, reminders and shopping lists.

- **Fight the frustration:** Listen carefully when your child talks about having difficulty with his homework. Encourage him to break down problems into small steps.

- **Set the right mood:** Make your home a place where it is easy for your child to learn. Keep books, magazines, catalogs and writing materials at easy reach. Make sure that your child has a place to study. This could be in the child's room, in the kitchen, or in another place where the lighting is good, and it's quiet. Be near enough to answer questions that your child has.

If your child does homework somewhere else (such as at his after school program or at a day care provider's home), be sure to discuss with them where and how the homework gets done. Ask them to provide a quiet, well-lit space for homework. Once your child is at home, go over his homework to make sure it is complete. Answer any questions he has about his work.

The example you set will make more of an impression than your words. The more interested you are in his homework, the more your child sees you learning, the more excited he will be about learning. Make sure your child sees you reading. Limit the amount and kind of TV you watch.

Limit your child's TV viewing to not more than 10 hours per week. Suggest programs that have useful tie-ins to schoolwork, such as shows about history, computers or animal life. Discuss these shows with your child. Help him see the connection to his school work.

- **Don't pinch hit:** Your child must learn to "face the music" for poor or incomplete work. While you should be actively involved with being sure your child does his homework, don't carry the whole load. Don't do the long division, write the essay or do the science project for your child. If you are getting overly involved in homework because of a concern that it is too difficult for your child, call or visit the child's teacher and share your concern.

- **Encourage independent growth:** Eventually a child must take charge of his own learning. This means that it is important for you to "let go" when your child pursues hobbies and starts reading for his own enjoyment.

  One way to encourage independent growth is to maintain the daily "quiet time" even during vacations and weekends. Introducing your child to hobbies, even something as simple as reading the cricket scores in the sports section of your newspaper, is a good way to make non-homework learning fun.

- **Use the school:** Get to know your child's teachers and what they expect. Compare your goals for your child to those of the teachers. Make sure that your child knows of your interest in his school. This will send the message that what he is doing is important.

  - Tell teachers of special events or any development at home, that may influence how your child does in school.

- Get answers to all of your questions about homework requirements, attendance policies, dress and conduct rules, discipline policies and curriculum guidelines.

  Talk with your child and find out what his concerns are. If you learn that your child feels ignored or "picked on" in the classroom, talk with the appropriate school official. If you can't find the time to visit in person, call the teachers or attach notes to homework your child is taking back to school.

Important Note

If the steps described here don't help your child, see if he suffers from a physical or behavior problem or learning disability. Talk with a medical doctor or other qualified professional for expert advice.

Signs that your child may need assistance:

- Your child has a hard time focusing on one thing—both at home and at school.

- Your child is doing well in many areas, but has one area that is very difficult. For example, she always gets B's in reading and writing, but is doing poorly in math.

- Your child is repeatedly "in trouble" – for disrupting class, not completing in-class work, or fighting at school.

- Your child reports that no one at school "likes his," and seems to have no real friends.

- You know your child could do better, but he "just doesn't apply himself" or "is just lazy."

- Your child complains that she cannot see the board clearly.

   - Your child has great difficulty in writing. For example, he can tell you what he wants to write, but can't seem to get it on paper.

   - Your child's handwriting is very poor, and does not improve.

   - Homework time has become a battle at home.

   - You have a feeling that "something" is getting in the way of your child's doing his best.

Checklist for Parents

Your child's learning: Make a daily checklist Clip and place it on your refrigerator or another spot where you will be sure to see it every day.

- Is a learning "quiet time" scheduled for my child today?

- How can I praise the effort and/or thinking of my child today?

- Have I clearly talked about what I expect? Have I avoided making excuses for low effort by my child?

- Can I praise a good effort?

- What will I read or write today to set a good example?

- How will I get relaxed before homework time so that I do not become impatient?

- Have I made it clear that my child (not me) is responsible for homework?

- Can I involve my child in a household activity today that will show the practical importance of learning?

- Have I encouraged my child to pursue a hobby, reading the newspaper or another independent activity?

- Did I remember to "sign off" on homework and attach a note if there is a problem?

✗ ✗ ✗

"To the world you are one person, *but to your child* you are **THE WORLD!**"

Make their world beautiful
&
fill it with **Love!**

SOURCES TO CONTACT FOR MORE INFORMATION

- **National Indian Education Association (NIEA)**

  110 Maryland Avenue, N.E.
  Suite 104
  Washington, D.C. 20002
  Phone: (202) 544-7290
  Fax: (202) 544-7293

  E-mail: niea@niea.org

- **India Development Gateway (InDG)**

  Centre for Development of Advanced Computing (CDAC)

  Jawaharlal Nehru Technological University (JNTU) Campus,

  Kukatpally, Hyderabad- 500085

  Phone No- +91 040-23150115

  Fax: 040-23150117

  E-Mail: indg@cdac.in

- **National Portal Secretariat**

3rd Floor, National Informatics Centre

A-Block, CGO Complex,

Lodhi Road, New Delhi - 110 003,   India

E-mail: indiaportal@gov.in

- **Counseling Association of India**

103 Satyam Mall, Mansi cross roads, Vastrapur, Ahmedabad- 380015

Phone number: (91)-8905573201

E-mail address: contact@counselingindia.org

- **Protection of Children against Corporal Punishment in Schools and Institutions**

Web site: http://indiacurrentaffairs.org/protection-of-children-against-corporal-punishment-in-schools-and-institutions/

- **Minds and Souls** in association with "Mother and Child Welfare and Research Foundation India (MAC)"

Miracles Astalavista & Numerologic

"Mother & Child Study Point"

114A/B, Ashutosh Mukherjee Road, 2nd Floor,

Kolkata - 700 025. West Bengal (India.)

Vodafone: +(91)-98308 88888, 98300 28888

Airtel: +(91)-98310 28888
Reliance: +(91)-93300 28888, 93390 52222
Web site: http://www.mindsandsouls.org

Understand Your Child: Teen and Child Personality Test

http://www.personalitylab.org/tests/bfi2_parent_outs.htm

                                                              ✗✗✗

The Books that will give you Knowledge, Awareness and Remove your Misconceptions

MAKE YOUR CHILD A RESPONSIBLE CITIZEN

Learn how to Make your Child Responsible effortlessly

Gullybaba Kids.com